FAR FROM THE
MADDING CROWD

Original by Thomas Hardy

Retold by Pauline Francis

READZONE

ReadZone Books Limited

First published in this edition 2017

Printed in Malta by Melita Press

Every attempt has been made by the Publisher to secure appropriate permissions for material reproduced in this book. If there has been any oversight we will be happy to rectify the situation in future editions or reprints. Written submissions should be made to the Publishers.

British Library Cataloguing in Publication Data (CIP) is available for this title.

ISBN 978 1 78322 640 5

Visit our website: www.readzonebooks.com

FAR FROM THE
MADDING CROWD

Introduction

Thomas Hardy was born in Dorset, in 1840. His father was a stonemason. He did not have enough money to send his son to university, so Thomas was apprenticed as an architect.

In 1874, he married Eleanor Gifford and designed a house for them called Max Gate. The house was close to Dorchester in Dorset, where he lived all his life.

Hardy saw himself as a poet rather than a novelist. However, his poetry was not published until after many of his well-known novels.

These novels include *Far from the Madding Crowd* (1874); *The Mayor of Casterbridge* (1886); *Tess of the d'Urbervilles* (1892) and *Jude the Obscure* (1895). In *Far from the Madding Crowd*, Hardy gave his beloved Dorset the fictional name of Wessex. He used this name in many of his novels.

Far from the Madding Crowd tells the story of Miss Bathsheba Everdene, a young woman who becomes a farmer, and how three different men fall in love with her. This novel of romance and tragedy is thought by many people to be his first masterpiece.

Thomas Hardy died in 1928, at the age of 87. His heart is buried in a churchyard close to Max Gate, but his ashes are buried in Poet's Corner, Westminster Abbey.

CHAPTER ONE

The Woman in Scarlet

One sunny December day, Farmer Gabriel Oak was walking his fields. He was a youngish man of twenty-eight who wore a wide-brimmed felt hat, leather boots and an old smock. Tucked inside his trouser waistband was his old silver watch.

Coming down the steep hill towards him was a yellow wagon drawn by two horses. It was laden with household goods and a young dark-haired woman, who wore a crimson jacket. It came to a halt. The waggoner had to go back up the hill to look for the tailgate of the wagon which had fallen off.

Now the wagon was silent, except for the canary singing in its cage and the purring of a cat in a wicker basket. The young woman looked around her to make sure that she was alone and opened a small oblong package next to her. It contained a mirror. She smiled at herself in it.

Gabriel Oak also smiled. 'She has no reason to look in that mirror,' he thought. 'She is not adjusting her clothes or her hair or her hat. She is simply looking at what beauty nature has given her.'

The young woman wrapped up the looking-glass as the waggoner returned and they drove on to the toll gate in the distance. Gabriel Oak could hear an argument. The gatekeeper wanted two more pence, which the woman refused to pay.

Gabriel Oak paid the two pence. The woman glanced carelessly at him and told her man to drive on. She did not thank him.

'That's a handsome woman,' the gatekeeper said.

'Yes, but she has her faults,' Gabriel replied. 'Vanity.'

***

A few days later, on the shortest day of the year, Gabriel Oak sat in his shepherd's hut, playing his flute. He had worked hard during the past year to lease a small sheep farm, and stock it with two hundred sheep. It was a giant step for Gabriel Oak. He still had to pay for some of the sheep, and it was important that the lambing of his ewes took place safely.

On his way to and from the ewes, Gabriel thought he saw a star in the sky. Then he realised it was a lantern light coming from an old shed on the side of the next hill. He made his way there and peeped inside to see a middle-aged woman tending a cow that had just calved.

A young woman, wrapped in a long, hooded cloak was helping her.

She yawned. 'I wish we were rich enough to pay a man

to do these things,' she said.

'As we are not, you must help if you stay with me,' the older woman said.

'I lost my hat on the way here,' the young woman said. 'The wind blew it over the hedge.'

As she spoke, the girl dropped her cloak, revealing her dark hair tumbling over a scarlet jacket.

Gabriel Oak recognised her.

'She owes me two pence,' he said to himself.

The two women left the hut, their lantern light sinking down the hill – and Gabriel Oak went back to his flock.

***

Just as dawn was breaking, Gabriel saw the young woman again. This time, she was riding a horse.

He remembered that she had lost her hat. He found it in a ditch, covered with leaves, and waited for her to pass so that he could return it. As she approached, she had to pass under a low branch. She lay flat on her back, her head over the horse's tail, her feet around its ears. Then she sat upright and rode on. Gabriel Oak saw that she had no side saddle and rode the pony like a man.

He approached her as she rode back from the mill with a bag of oats. He blushed as he held out her hat. She did not.

'It flew away last night,' she said.

'Yes, at one o'clock in the morning,' Gabriel Oak replied.

'How did you know that?' she asked.

'I was there,' he said.

'You are Farmer Oak, are you not?'

'I am,' he replied.

Five mornings and nights passed. The young woman came to feed the cows. But she never came near him. Gabriel Oak had committed the worst sin of all and it had offended her.

He had spied on her.

***

One evening, a sharp frost fell. As the milking-hour drew near, Gabriel Oak kept his usual watch on the cowshed. But he was so cold that he went inside his hut, blocking up the door and the ventilation holes with straw as he heaped up the fire.

'I'll sit here a moment to get myself warm,' he thought.

He did not know how long he was unconscious. When he opened his eyes, it was dusk. His dog was howling and somebody was loosening his neckerchief. His head, which lay on somebody's lap, ached badly.

He looked up to see the face of the young woman.

'Whatever is the matter?' he asked.

'Nothing now,' she replied. 'But you might have suffocated in this hut of yours, except that I heard your dog howling and scratching the door.'

'I believe you saved my life,' Gabriel muttered. 'I thank thee.'

He went to kiss her hand, but she withdrew it.

'Now find out my name,' she teased him as she left.

CHAPTER TWO

A Terrible Accident

The girl was called Bathsheba Everdene and she had come to stay with her aunt. But when the cow stopped giving milk for the winter, she did not come up to the cowshed any more.

Gabriel Oak missed her and knew that he had fallen in love with her.

'I'll make her my wife,' he told himself. 'If I don't, I shall be good for nothing.'

He decided to take her a motherless lamb as a gift. He dressed smartly in a flowered waistcoat, cut a new walking stick from a willow and made his way to her aunt's cottage. She said that Bathsheba was out. Gabriel told her that he wanted to marry Bathsheba, only to learn that she had other young men interested in her. As he made his way home, Bathsheba ran to catch up with him.

'I haven't a sweetheart at all,' she said.

Gabriel blushed – and misunderstood why she had run after him.

'When we be married, I am sure I can work twice as hard,' he said.

'Why, Farmer Oak, I never said I was going to marry you,' Bathsheba replied. 'I only wanted to say I didn't like what my aunt told you. I do not want you to think I belong to any man.'

'But might you marry me?' Gabriel persisted. 'At home by the fire, whenever you look up, there I shall be – and whenever I look up, there will be you.'

'I don't want to marry you,' Bathsheba said. 'I don't love you. No, it wouldn't do, Mr Oak. I want someone to tame me and you would never be able to do that, I know.'

'Very well,' he replied. 'Then I'll ask you no more.'

***

Gabriel learned soon afterwards that Bathsheba had left the neighbourhood and was now living near a village called Weatherbury, more than twenty miles away. Now that she had gone – and he did not know how long for – his love for her only ran deeper.

One fine night, Gabriel went to sleep, leaving his dogs up on the hill feasting on a dead sheep. Early the next morning, he heard the ring of a sheep bell, which sounded strange. It told him that the sheep was running very fast. He dressed quickly and ran through the fog to the hill. Most of his sheep had disappeared from the hillside. Only fifty ewes and their lambs remained in their pen.

The misty hill rang with Gabriel's voice. He went to the very top, where it dropped to a deep chalk-pit, and peered through the broken fence, faint from fear. Below him lay the dead and dying bodies of his sheep.

He was not insured. It had taken every bit of his savings to buy his flock. Gabriel Oak put his face in his hands and muttered, 'Thank God I am not married! What would *she* have done in the poverty now coming upon me!'

After Gabriel Oak had paid all his debts, he had nothing more than the clothes he stood up in – and his flute.

***

Two months later, in February, he made his way to Casterbridge, to the hiring fair. There he waited with three hundred hearty labourers, all seeking work. Gabriel Oak stood, paler than he used to be; but dignified and calm. Nobody hired him. He spent his last money on a shepherd's crook and clothes and played his flute. Then he set off for another fair, close to Weatherbury, where Bathsheba had gone.

Just outside the town, he saw fire in the sky, coming from a large hay stack, threatening the others around it. Gabriel ran to help and stopped the fire spreading.

'I might be able to find work here,' he told himself.

Two women rode in to see the damage.

'Where is your master, the farmer?' Gabriel asked one of them.

'Tisn't a master, tis a mistress, shepherd,' she replied.

'Lately come here and took her uncle's farm,' a bystander added. 'That's her, over there, on the pony.'

Gabriel Oak, smudged with smoke, his grimysmock burnt into holes and his shepherd's crook charred, lifted his hat and stepped close to the woman's feet.

'Do you want a shepherd, ma'am?' he asked.

The woman lifted her veil.

It was Bathsheba Everdene. She did not know whether to be amused or embarrassed.

'Yes, I do,' she said coldly.

***

On his way to the village inn to find lodgings, Gabriel Oak met a young girl in the churchyard. She looked so thin and fragile that he made her take a shilling.

He received a warm welcome at the inn from men who had known his grandparents and parents. They asked him to play his flute. There was gossip, too. Miss Everdene had sacked her manager, Pennyworth, for theft after the fire – and her youngest servant, Fanny, had gone missing.

Bathsheba called a meeting of all her farm workers, asking them if they wished to stay on and work for her.

'Do you quite understand your duties, Gabriel Oak?' Bathsheba asked.

'Quite well, I thank you, Miss Everdene,' he replied, dismayed by the coolness of her manner. 'If I don't, I'll enquire.'

Nobody in the room would have guessed that they already knew one another.

Just before the end of the meeting, news came that the servant, Fanny, had run away with a soldier from a nearby regiment.

At the end of the meeting, Bathsheba rose from her chair saying, 'You have a mistress instead of a master. I don't yet know my talents in farming, but I shall do my best. If you serve me well, I shall serve you well. I shall be up before you are awake. I shall astonish you all.'

With these words, Bathsheba swept out of the hall in her black silk dress, its hem picking up a few pieces of straw on the way.

CHAPTER THREE

The Valentine

Nothing could be bleaker than the military barracks a few miles north of Weatherbury. It was snowing heavily. There was a small figure down by the river, throwing snow against one of the windows. A soldier opened it.

'Who's there?' he called out.

'Is that Sergeant Troy?' a small voice asked.

'Yes,' he replied. 'Who are you?'

'Oh, Frank, don't you know me? Your sweetheart, Fanny Robin? You said I was to come to you.'

'Fanny?' the soldier said, utterly astonished.

'You *are* glad to see me, Frank?' she asked.

'Oh yes – of course,' he replied, uncertain.

'When shall we be married, Frank?' She began to cry. 'I love you so, and you said you would marry me... and... I ... I...'

'Don't cry,' he said.

'Have you asked permission from your officer?' she asked.

'Not yet. I'll come to you when I have.'

Fanny Robin left. She did not hear the laughter that burst from within the room.

***

Bathsheba Everdene put in her first public appearance as a farmer the following market day in Casterbridge. She had brought samples of her grains to the Corn Exchange, where she knew several of the farmers. In arguing the price, she was firm and polite.

The farmers knew she was headstrong, having decided to run the farm without a manager. They were proud of her, but – amongst themselves – they bet that she would soon be married.

Bathsheba herself felt that everybody was staring at her. She noticed that there was one farmer, a man of about forty, who hardly glanced at her.

His name was Mr Boldwood. He was the tenant of her neighbouring farm – Little Weatherbury Farm. He was rich and unmarried. And he had called on Bathsheba already, only to find her not at home.

***

It was February the thirteenth, the day before Valentine's Day. Bathsheba was bored – it was a cold Sunday afternoon – and she asked Liddy, her servant and companion, to sit with her.

'Did you see Farmer Boldwood in church this morning?'

Liddy asked. 'He didn't look at you once.'

'Why should he?' Bathsheba asked.

'Well, everybody else did,' Liddy replied.

Bathsheba laughed. 'Dear me,' she said, 'I've forgotten the valentine I bought yesterday.'

'For Farmer Boldwood?'

'No, it's for one of the little village children.'

'It would be fun to send it to Farmer Boldwood,' Liddy said.

'So, the richest and most important man in the parish does not look at me,' Bathsheba thought. 'Yes, I *shall* send it to him.'

How she and Liddy laughed as they sealed the letter for Boldwood. Only when the wax had set on the seal did Bathsheba read its message: MARRY ME. But it did not stop her sending it.

Mr Boldwood could not believe his eyes.

He put the letter on his mantelpiece and stared at it. It looked like a woman's handwriting. *Who* could have written it?

The frost was hard when Boldwood went out for a walk, the valentine in his pocket. He met the postman coming up the hill with a letter for Gabriel Oak, and he offered to take it to him.

Gabriel Oak did not recognise the handwriting on his letter either. He opened it at once and read:

"Dear Friend

I do not know your name. I write to thank you for your kindness the night I left Weatherbury. I also return the shilling I owe you. All has ended well and I am happy to tell you that I am to be married to Sergeant Troy, of the 11th Dragoon Guards.

I would be obliged if you would keep the contents of this letter a secret.

I am your sincere well-wisher, Fanny Robin"

He showed the letter to Boldwood.

'What sort of man is this Sergeant Troy?' Gabriel asked.

'Mmm... not one to inspire much hope, I'm afraid,' Mr Boldwood replied. 'I doubt he will ever marry her. Poor, silly Fanny.'

He took out his valentine and asked Gabriel Oak if he recognised the handwriting.

'Yes,' Gabriel said. 'That is the hand of Miss Bathsheba Everdene.'

***

There was a church close to the army barracks and a young soldier in red uniform stood waiting for his bride.

'I wonder where she is,' the congregation whispered.

The clock ticked on. The congregation laughed silently, but the soldier stood still, cap in hand. At last, he walked out of the church into the little square. There he met a woman coming towards him, her face full of terror.

'Oh, Frank,' she said. 'I've been waiting at the wrong church. Shall we marry tomorrow now?'

'You have made a fool of me,' the soldier said.

'When will it be?' she cried.

'Ah, only God knows,' he said.

And the soldier – whose name was Troy – walked rapidly away from her.

CHAPTER FOUR

Misunderstandings

On Saturday, Mr Boldwood went to Casterbridge Corn Exchange as usual. There he saw Bathsheba, the woman who now disturbed his sleep.

He studied every detail of her face and figure – and he found her very beautiful.

'Why did this woman choose a seal that said MARRY ME?' he asked himself.

Bathsheba knew that he was watching her, and she felt guilty for teasing him with a valentine.

'I shall apologise when I have the chance to speak to him,' she told herself.

***

By early summer, Boldwood had grown used to being in love with Bathsheba Everdene. At last, he made up his mind to go and speak to her. She and Gabriel Oak were down in the meadow full of buttercups, washing sheep in the pond.

'I have come to make you an offer of marriage,' he said. 'I love you and my life is a burden without you. I should not have spoken out if you had not given me hope.'

'O, that valentine!' she said. 'I should never have sent it, sir. Forgive my thoughtlessness, I beg you. I have not fallen in love with you.'

'I fear I might be too old for you,' Boldwood continued. 'I am forty-one. But I can take care of you more than any man of your age. May I speak to you again on this subject? May I hope?'

'No, do not hope,' she replied.

'I shall wait,' he replied.

She turned to go. Boldwood stood staring at the ground, like a man who did not know where he was.

***

The next day, Bathsheba met Gabriel by the grindstone at the bottom of the garden where he was sharpening his shears. She decided to speak to him.

'You turn the stone, I'll hold the shears,' she said.

When the wheel began to turn she asked, 'What is your opinion of my conduct yesterday?'

'That it is unworthy of any thoughtful woman,' Gabriel Oak replied.

Bathsheba's face coloured to an angry crimson.

'You should not have played such a trick on Boldwood, Bathsheba,' he continued.

'Miss Everdene, you mean,' she said with dignity.

'So you think I am unworthy because I did not marry you?' she cried.

'I have long given up thinking of that matter,' he replied quietly. 'I know it was rudeness to say what I just said, but I thought it may do good.'

'I cannot allow any man to criticise my behaviour,' Bathsheba said. 'Please leave my farm at the end of the week.' Her lower lip trembled.

'I shall go now, Miss Everdene,' he replied.

He collected his shears and left the farm with quiet dignity.

***

It was only a day later when a group of men came running to Upper Farm, just as Bathsheba was leaving for church.

'Whatever is the matter?' she asked.

'About sixty sheep!' one of the men cried. 'They've broken the fence and got into a field of clover and now they're swelling up with gas. They'll soon be dead.'

'Why have you wasted time coming to me when you should be trying to save them?' she shouted.

Bathsheba looked beautiful in her anger as she ran to her sheep. Some were already foaming at the mouth. There was only one cure – the wind in the sheep's stomach would have to be released by a skilled shepherd.

'There's only one man who can do it!' one of them cried. 'Shepherd Oak.'

'How dare you mention *that* man's name in front of me?' Bathsheba cried. 'Farmer Boldwood will know what to do.'

'No, he won't, ma'am,' the man told her. 'He had the same trouble and Farmer Gabriel saved his ewes.'

'Never will I send for *him*!' Bathsheba told herself. She watched one of the ewes topple over and die. Then she was forced to change her mind. But Gabriel would not come when he received her letter. He said she must ask more kindly.

Bathsheba wiped her eyes and wrote another note. But at the bottom she added these words: *"Do not desert me, Gabriel!"*

Gabriel Oak came at once. He saved forty-nine sheep that terrible Sunday. Bathsheba lost only five in all.

'Gabriel, will you stay with me then?' she asked, smiling.

'I will,' Gabriel said.

And she smiled again.

***

It was the first day of June, and the countryside was bursting with blossom, catkins and trees with young leaves.

Sheep were being sheared in the Great Barn. The doors had been flung open so the sun shone on the thick oak floor. At one end of the barn stood Bathsheba, watching carefully to make sure that none of her sheep was cut during the shearing.

Poor Gabriel Oak. He liked having Bathsheba so close to him, but he had no wish for conversation. It was she who did all the talking.

Suddenly, Farmer Boldwood strode into the barn. He and Bathsheba talked quietly. Then they went outside, and Gabriel was left alone for at least a quarter of an hour. When Bathsheba returned, she was wearing a green riding outfit, tightly fitted at the waist.

As Gabriel Oak watched them get ready to ride off together, he cut the sheep he was shearing. It fell to the ground. Bathsheba saw what had happened and came running in.

'O Gabriel, what have you done?' she cried.

But in her heart, she knew that she was to blame for distracting him.

***

A large table was set out on the lawn beside the farmhouse for the shearing supper. The end of the table rested on the parlour windowsill. Bathsheba sat inside the window at the head of the table, facing her men. She asked Gabriel Oak to sit by her until Mr Boldwood arrived. Then she asked Gabriel to give him his seat.

They made merry and sang until dusk. Towards the end of the evening, the workers insisted that Bathsheba sing for them.

'Have you brought your flute, Gabriel?' she asked.

'Yes, Miss Everdene.'

'Play to my singing then,' she said.

Gabriel Oak stood to Bathsheba's right. Mr Boldwood stood to her left, singing with Bathsheba.

Then everybody went home – except for Mr Boldwood. Bathsheba stood behind a chair in her sitting room and he was kneeling in it, holding her hands.

'I will try to love you,' she was saying. 'As you say you will be away from now until the harvest, give me those few weeks to decide. But remember what I say now – I can't promise you, Mr Boldwood.'

'It is enough, Miss Everdene,' he replied. 'Now I bid you goodnight.'

'Oh dear, he has worn himself out with love for my sake,' Bathsheba thought.

But, secretly, she was delighted at her success.

CHAPTER FIVE

An Unexpected Meeting

The most important part of Bathsheba's job, since she had decided not to employ a manager, was to see that all was right and safe for the night. She liked to be almost invisible, so she carried a dark lantern, opening it only when she needed to peer into a hidden corner.

Her way back to the house was through a small plantation of young fir trees. It was a dark and gloomy spot; but Bathsheba was never afraid. However, as she entered the trees that night, she thought she could hear the rustle of footsteps.

A figure passed close by. Something tugged at Bathsheba's skirt and she could not move. Almost losing her balance, she put out her hand and felt clothes and buttons.

'Have I hurt you, my friend?' a man's voice said.

'No,' Bathsheba said, shrinking back.

'Let me open your lantern,' he said.

The light burst out and Bathsheba saw a soldier, brilliant in brass and scarlet. His spurs had caught in the hem of her skirt.

'I'll unfasten you, ma'am,' he said.

It was difficult to do and they had to work at it together,

the lantern placed on the ground between them.

'Thank you for the sight of such a beautiful face,' the soldier said.

Bathsheba blushed. 'It was unwillingly shown,' she said. She was quickly losing patience with the soldier.

'Who are you?' she asked.

'Sergeant Troy,' he replied. 'There, it's done, although I wish we could have stayed tied together forever!'

Bathsheba made her way home angrily and told Liddy what had happened. But when she went to bed, she thought about the man she had just met.

'Mr Boldwood has never told me once that I am beautiful,' she said to herself.

***

Sergeant Troy was a man who only lived in the present. He did not think very deeply, but took whatever came his way. It was his habit to lie to women in order to make himself popular with them.

It was haymaking time and Bathsheba had gone to the fields to check that all was well. She spotted Troy's scarlet jacket at once.

He paused in his work. 'I must apologise for being so outspoken last night,' he said. 'I used to help your uncle in these fields when I was a boy. I grew up here and went to school in Casterbridge. I came to help today for the pleasure of it.'

'I suppose I must thank you for that,' she replied.

'I would rather have curses from you than kisses from any other woman,' Troy said.

Bathsheba was speechless. She turned away.

Troy followed her, begging her forgiveness. 'Other men must surely have said the same thing to you,' he said.

'Not to my face, as you do,' she replied.

'I do not want to be drawn any further into this conversation,' she told herself.

But she was, until she forced herself to say, 'Mind you do not speak to me in that way, or in any other, unless I speak to you.'

'O, Miss Bathsheba, that is too hard!' Troy said. 'You will *never* speak to me as I shall not be here long. My regiment will be ordered out within the month.'

She tried to leave, anxious about the time and he pressed her to take his watch, which had belonged to his father. Bathsheba became agitated and refused. But she promised to let him work in her fields.

Bathsheba made her way home, almost in tears.

'O what have I done?' she cried.

CHAPTER SIX
Bathsheba falls in Love

There were bees swarming in Bathsheba's garden. She had prepared her hive with herbs and honey, but they had swarmed into a nearby tree. There was nobody at home. It was the middle of haymaking, and even Liddy had gone to help in the fields.

Bathsheba put on gloves and her hat and veil and started to climb the ladder she had set against the tree. She wanted to encourage the bees to fly to her hive.

She had just started to climb when a man's voice called out, 'Miss Everdene, let me assist you. You should not attempt such a thing alone.'

It was Sergeant Troy, just opening the garden gate. He offered to help and Bathsheba could not help but laugh as he dressed in her veiled hat and gloves. As they began to talk, she mentioned the sword exercises that soldiers must practise at the barracks. He offered to demonstrate them for her.

***

They met in a fern-filled hollow of a hill opposite Bathsheba's farm. It was eight o'clock on midsummer night and everything was touched with gold. Troy asked her to stand still as he flashed his sword around her. Sunlight caught the blade as it whistled around her head.

'You have a loose lock of hair that needs tidying,' Troy said, cutting it with his sword. 'I must leave you now, and I take this in remembrance of you.'

Bathsheba saw him stoop to pick up the lock of hair he had severed and he put it inside his coat. She felt powerless to prevent him.

'He is altogether too much for me,' she thought. 'He is like a strong wind that has taken away my breath.'

Troy drew close to her and kissed her. Then he was quickly on his way, leaving Bathsheba in tears.

It was then that Bathsheba realised that she loved Troy. And since she was a strong woman, she loved him more than a weak one would. She knew that she had thrown away her strength. She loved as a child would and did not think of the consequences. She forgot his weaknesses, was aware only of what she loved.

As for Gabriel Oak, she had seen only his weaknesses. His virtues were hidden as deep as metal in a mine. And, strangely, she had never spoken to Liddy about Troy, as she had confided in her about Mr Boldwood.

And what about Gabriel Oak? He saw her infatuation for Troy and considered it unfair to Mr Boldwood, who was now away from home.

'I shall speak to her about it,' he told himself.

One evening, at dusk, he took the same path as she did and met her by the tall wheat.

'It is rather late,' he said, 'and there are some bad characters about.'

'I never meet them,' she replied.

'And as the man who would naturally come to meet you is away,' he continued.

'Ah, yes, Mr Boldwood,' she said, walking on, 'but he does not usually come to meet me. I do not know what you mean.' There was no sound except the rustle of her dress against the corn.

'They say you will marry him when he returns,' Gabriel Oak said.

'Then they say what is not true,' she replied quickly. 'I have never cared for him and I shall tell him so when he returns.'

'I wish you had never met that Sergeant Troy, miss,' he sighed.

'Why?'

'He is not good enough for thee,' Oak replied. 'He has no conscience at all. I ask you *not* to trust him, mistress.'

Bathsheba was furious. Her cheeks flushed angrily.

'He is as good as anybody in this parish,' she said. 'He goes to church.'

'I fear nobody ever saw him there,' he said. 'I never did.'

'That's because he enters by the old tower door to sit at the back of the gallery,' Bathsheba replied. 'He told me so.'

Gabriel Oak was grieved to find how much Bathsheba trusted Troy. He tried to steady his voice as he reminded her how much he loved her and he always would.

'You mean more to me than anything,' he said. 'I beg you to consider that you will be safe in Mr Boldwood's hands, not in this soldier's.'

She lessened her anger, seeing that Gabriel Oak was concerned only for her welfare. But she resented his criticism of Sergeant Troy.

'I wish you to go elsewhere,' she said.

'This is nonsense,' Gabriel replied calmly. 'And the second time you have pretended to dismiss me.'

'*Pretended*?' Bathsheba said. 'You should go – now.'

'How can I?' he asked, 'when you have no manager. I know I interfere but your ways are so provoking.'

'Well, you can stay if that is what you wish,' Bathsheba replied. 'Now leave me alone. I don't ask it as a mistress. I order it as a woman.'

'Certainly I will, Miss Everdene,' Gabriel Oak replied.

He worried about her safety for they were almost at the top of a dark and bleak hill.

'Why is she so keen to be rid of me?' he asked himself.

The answer was clear. Another figure came into view,

just a shape in the dusk – Sergeant Troy.

As Gabriel Oak passed the church on his way home, he looked at the little door that Troy used to enter the church. Thick ivy grew from the wall across it. It had not been opened since Sergeant Troy had come back to Weatherbury.

CHAPTER SEVEN

Troy has the Upper Hand

Bathsheba decided that she would not wait until Mr Boldwood returned home. That same night, she wrote to him, telling him that she could not marry him. Two days later, when she was walking over nearby Yalbury Hill, she came across the very man she hoped to avoid – Mr Boldwood.

'He does not look happy,' she said to herself. 'My letter has affected him deeply.'

'O, Bathsheba, have pity on me!' Boldwood burst out. 'Remember how you once encouraged me with that valentine at a time when I knew nothing of you.'

'It was a childish game,' Bathsheba replied. 'And I regret it now.' She looked him straight in the eye. 'I promised you nothing, Mr Boldwood.'

'I know where your love has gone now,' he replied. 'Why didn't Troy leave you alone? He stole you in my absence. Deny that he has kissed you.'

'Yes, he has kissed me,' she replied slowly.

'Then I curse him,' Boldwood said. 'I'll punish him! Bathsheba, I beg you, keep him away from me.'

He walked off into the twilight, leaving Bathsheba to hide her face in her hands. She missed Troy, who was in

Bath visiting friends.

'I *must* see him,' she thought.

Bathsheba left for Bath almost immediately.

Two or three weeks passed by. News came that Bathsheba had been seen walking in Bath, on the arm of a soldier *and* dressed in fine clothes.

At last, she returned to Weatherbury. Gabriel Oak felt an exquisite relief when he saw Liddy helping her from her carriage. He went home with a lighter heart, passing Mr Boldwood on the way. Hearing the news, Boldwood went over to see Bathsheba. He wanted to apologise and beg her forgiveness, but Bathsheba refused to see him.

Boldwood did not hurry home. He was walking through Weatherbury when he heard the sound of a carriage and saw a lamp lighting up the face of Sergeant Troy. The soldier jumped down, picked up his bag and walked out of the village in the direction of the farm. Boldwood went after him.

'I am William Boldwood,' he said. 'I want to speak to you about the woman you have wronged.'

'I am astonished by your cheek,' Troy replied, continuing on.

'You *will* listen to me,' Boldwood said. 'I am the only person in the village, apart from Gabriel Oak, who knows of your attachment to Fanny Robin. You should marry *her.*'

'I suppose I ought, but I cannot,' Troy replied. He was about to say something else, but he stopped himself. 'I am too poor.'

'If you had not turned up, I most certainly would be engaged to Miss Everdene by now,' Boldwood said. 'Marry Fanny. I'll make it worth your while. I'll pay you well – and Fanny. Yes, leave Weatherbury tonight.'

'I do like Fanny best,' Troy replied. 'I shall do as you ask.'

They heard footsteps on the path. It was Bathsheba. She was so happy to see Troy that Boldwood changed his mind. How could he be responsible for making Bathsheba unhappy?

Troy sent Bathsheba inside to wait for him. Now Boldwood begged Troy to marry *her*.

How Troy enjoyed watching William Boldwood suffer! At last he put him out of his misery. He handed him a newspaper, showing the announcement of the marriage between himself and Bathsheba in Bath.

'You devil!' Boldwood cried. 'I'll punish you yet.'

***

Very early the next morning – at the time of sun and dew – Gabriel Oak was making his way to work. He saw Bathsheba's window flung open. A man, a scarlet jacket flung loosely round his shoulders, was looking down on the garden.

'She has married him,' Gabriel said to himself. He leaned on the gate, his face as deathly white as a corpse.

Farmer Boldwood also rode by and Gabriel Oak saw that the grief etched on the man's face was equal to his own.

***

It was the end of August and the night of the Harvest Supper. There was thunder in the air, but the haystacks were not covered. Gabriel Oak sent word to Troy that there would be rain; but he paid no attention.

During the supper, Troy gave the workers bottles of brandy, although Bathsheba begged him not to do it. By the time the storm broke, all the men were asleep in the barn – drunk.

It was Gabriel Oak who had to cover up the hay all by himself, until Bathsheba came out to help him.

As for Farmer Boldwood, he took no steps to protect his harvest.

CHAPTER EIGHT

Fanny Robin and Child

One Saturday evening, at the end of October, Bathsheba and her husband were on their way home. She was sitting in the gig. Sergeant Troy walked alongside, except that he was no longer a soldier in the army. He had paid for his discharge with his wife's money.

He still looked like a soldier, though, with his upright walk and moustache.

They had been to the horse races and he was cursing because it had rained – and he had lost a lot of money.

'O, Frank, it is cruel,' Bathsheba was saying. 'It is foolish to take away my money so. We shall have to leave the farm if we cannot pay the rent.'

'Humbug,' Troy said. 'Now, turn on the waterworks. Why, Bathsheba, you have lost all the sparkle you used to have.'

A woman appeared at the brow of the hill. She was very poorly dressed and asked what time the workhouse in Casterbridge closed.

'I do not know,' he said, startled by the sight of her.

The woman looked up at him, screamed and fell to the ground. Troy sent Bathsheba on ahead and gave the woman the few coins he had.

'Why didn't you write to me, Fanny?' he asked. 'Go to the workhouse tonight, but meet me on Grey's Bridge on Monday, at ten o' clock. I will bring all the money I can. I'll see to that, Fanny. I'm not a brute.'

'Who was that woman?' Bathsheba asked her husband when he came home.

'Just somebody I know by sight,' he replied.

***

On Monday morning, Bathsheba and Troy quarrelled again because he asked her for twenty pounds. Bathsheba had also caught sight of a lock of hair inside his watch as he kept checking the time.

She cried after her husband had left. Then she went out to her work. She saw Boldwood and Gabriel speaking in the distance to the man who brought her apples.

Then Boldwood and Gabriel left, and the man continued towards her with his wheelbarrow of fruit.

'Do you have a message for me, Joseph?' she asked.

'You'll never see Fanny Robin no more, ma'am,' he replied. 'She's dead – at the workhouse. She were that worn out and starved, I think. Mr Boldwood's going to bring her back to bury her.'

'He'll do no such thing!' Bathsheba cried. 'She was my uncle's servant. Go to Mr Boldwood and say that Mrs

Troy will fetch back her servant. And, Joseph, put some flowers on the coffin. Poor Fanny! I thought she had gone away. I wish I'd known. How long has she been back?'

'A day or two,' he replied.

'Has she walked this way?'

'She passed by Weatherbury on Saturday night, ma'am,' he said.

Bathsheba had turned deadly pale.

'I wonder why Gabriel didn't bring me the message himself,' she thought.

***

Fanny Robin's coffin was brought to the farm ready for burial. Gabriel Oak, wishing to spare Bathsheba any further anguish, took a cloth and walked over to the coffin. Scrawled in chalk on the lid were the words: *Fanny Robin and child.*

Very carefully, he rubbed out the words *and child*.

Gossip came to Bathsheba's ears as she sat up late waiting for her husband to return – that Fanny Robin had had a child. She made her way to the room where the coffin stood and opened the lid.

She wailed. Her tears fell fast beside the dead mother and child in the coffin. Fanny's face was framed by her yellow hair and there was no doubt that it was the lock

Troy kept in his watch. She took flowers from a vase and laid them around Fanny's head. She forgot time, life, where she was, what she was doing.

A door slammed. Then Troy was standing in the doorway, watching her. Bathsheba gazed back wildly.

'Who is dead?' he cried.

She tried to pass him. He caught hold of her arm and together, they looked down into the coffin. The candle lit the features of both mother and child. Troy dropped his wife's hand and froze.

'Do you know her?' Bathsheba asked.

'I do,' Troy replied.

'Is it *her*?' she cried.

'It is.'

Troy was gradually sinking forward on to his knees so that he could kiss Fanny. Bathsheba flung her arms around his neck, clung to him wildly.

'Don't kiss them! O, Frank, I can't bear it,' she cried. 'I love you better than she did. Kiss me, Frank. You will kiss me too!'

Troy stared at her in astonishment and pushed her away.

'I will not kiss you,' he said. 'You are nothing to me,' he said cruelly. 'Our marriage means nothing. I am not yours.'

Bathsheba ran from the room. She spent the night under the old oak tree along the road. At dawn, she stood up, brushing the red and golden leaves from her clothes and saw Liddy coming towards her.

'I shall not come indoors yet, Liddy,' she whispered, because the damp had made her voice hoarse. 'Perhaps I never will!'

Liddy came back with hot tea and they walked in the wood until they knew that Fanny had been taken to be buried.

'I shall go back now, Liddy,' Bathsheba said. 'I shall stand my ground, not become a runaway wife, whom everybody pities. I shall make my room in the attic.'

Later, she visited the churchyard and wept when she saw Fanny Robin's headstone:

ERECTED BY FRANCIS TROY
IN LOVING MEMORY OF FANNY ROBIN

***

Troy did not show himself all that day. He spent the twenty pounds on the best headstone he could buy for Fanny and fell asleep on her grave. Then he left Weatherbury. He was bored with life on the farm with Bathsheba, and full of remorse for little Fanny Robin.

Troy headed towards the south coast.

His spirits rose as he reached the sea. He undressed and

plunged into a pool between two rocks. Unknown to him, there was a strong current and Troy found himself swept out to sea. He tried again and again to swim back to shore, but with no success.

Slowly, the tide was pulling him out to sea.

CHAPTER NINE

Murder!

At first, Bathsheba was relieved that her husband had left Weatherbury. Then she worried about her future at Upper Farm. Her uncle had insisted that she became the tenant, although the agent for the estate had doubts because of her youth and beauty.

'What if I cannot pay the rent on rent day,' she thought. 'They will show no pity for me now.'

That Saturday, Bathsheba went to market for the first time since her marriage.

A man was looking for her and she overheard him say, 'I am looking for Mrs Troy. I have some unfortunate news for her. Her husband has drowned. They found his clothes on the beach.'

'No, it cannot be true,' Bathsheba cried.

She would have fainted if Mr Boldwood had not caught her by the arm. He carried her to the nearest inn, where she asked to go home. Liddy insisted on finding mourning clothes for her.

'No, no. He is alive, Liddy,' she cried. 'I know it. They have not found his body.'

But later that night, sitting by the fire, Bathsheba could not help but wonder if Troy had decided to join Fanny Robin.

It was all she could do to stop herself throwing Fanny's lock of yellow hair into the flames.

***

Winter came on quickly. Bathsheba kept the farm going and made Gabriel Oak her manager. Farmer Boldwood asked Gabriel Oak to oversee his own neglected farm, in return for a small share of the profit. After Troy's death, he had begun to hope again that Bathsheba might consider marrying him. By law, she would be declared a widow after seven years' absence.

It was soon time for the Greenhill Fair, the biggest and merriest sheep fair in South Wessex. Bathsheba's sheep and those of Farmer Boldwood sold well. On another part of the hill, a large tent was being erected. This was for the performance of a show: Dick Turpin and his faithful horse, Black Bess. Behind the large tent were two small dressing tents for performers. In one of them was a man putting on his boots.

Troy.

How had he escaped that strong tide? A ship had appeared in the distance. Sailors had seen him against the setting sun and hauled him aboard. Troy decided to join the ship's crew, working his passage to the United States. There he had earned a precarious living teaching sword exercises, fencing and boxing. It was a hard life and he did not like being short of money.

'I can always return to the comforts of my farm if I choose,' he used to say to himself.

At last, he did decide to return to England, landing at Liverpool. But he put off visiting Weatherbury, knowing that he would receive a cold welcome.

'Bathsheba is not a woman to be made a fool of,' he thought. 'And Fanny will always be between us.'

In the July before the Greenhill Fair, Troy fell in with a travelling circus. He excelled in horsemanship and shooting, so the Dick Turpin show was prepared especially for him. It was by chance that he came to Greenhill.

When Bathsheba had sold all her sheep, she was free to wander. She entered the show tent. Troy saw her just before he was due to perform. How beautiful she was! How surprised he was by his feelings for her!

He managed to perform without being recognised. Afterwards, he put on a long beard and walked about. He was able to see Bathsheba close-up, in the tea booth with Mr Boldwood. Troy was filled with a desire to claim her again for his wife.

Suddenly, Pennyworth appeared. He was Bathsheba's former farm manager who had been sacked for theft.

'Excuse me, ma'am, I have some private information, for your ear alone,' he whispered.

'I cannot hear it now,' she said coldly. 'Write it down.'

He wrote: *Your husband is here. I have seen him.*

Then he folded up the paper and gave it to Bathsheba, who held it in her left hand as she finished her tea.

Troy cursed. He had no doubt that the note referred to him. Troy slipped his arm under the canvas and snatched it from her hand. Then he ran smiling into the darkness as Bathsheba screamed.

'I must make sure that Pennyworth does not speak to her again,' Troy said to himself.

He approached Pennyworth as he was listening to a fiddler and whispered in his ear. The ex-manager nodded and they left the fair together, heading for Weatherbury.

***

Mr Boldwood offered to escort Bathsheba back to her farm. He rode alongside her in the moonlight. He could not help asking if she would ever marry again.

'I may not be a widow,' Bathsheba replied. 'I think you are forgetting, Mr Boldwood, that my husband's death was never proved.'

They travelled on in silence for a while.

Once again, Boldwood persisted in his talk of marriage. He asked Bathsheba to promise to marry him in six years' time, if her husband's death was not proved.

Afraid of his anger, she agreed. But she confided in Gabriel Oak.

'I believe that if I don't give my word, he'll go out of his mind,' she said.

Bathsheba's promise invigorated Mr Boldwood. He held a Christmas party which was the talk of the village. Bathsheba was not happy, because she knew that it was being given in her honour.

Gabriel Oak was pleased to see the change in Farmer Boldwood. He was wearing a new jacket, and he clutched a ring in a box as he made his way downstairs. At exactly the same time, Troy – heavily disguised in a long coat and hat – began to walk towards the Boldwood farm.

'There she is with plenty of money and a home and a farm, and here I am living from hand to mouth,' he told himself.

Bathsheba was feeling very uncomfortable. Boldwood had slipped the engagement ring on her finger and she only wanted to go home. She was preparing to leave during a pause in the dancing when a stranger arrived and asked for Mrs Troy. He entered, wrapped up to his eyes. Some recognised him, although Boldwood did not. Troy turned down his coat collar and faced Boldwood. Bathsheba sank on to the lowest step of the stairs, as pale as death.

'Bathsheba, I come here for you!' Troy cried.

She did not move.

He commanded her to come. Then he pulled her to him, pinching her arm. Bathsheba sank back, giving a low scream. This was followed by the deafening sound of a gunshot that stupefied them all as the room filled with thick smoke. Boldwood had seized a gun from over the fireplace and discharged a bullet.

Troy fell dead.

Boldwood crossed the room, kissed Bathsheba's hand and disappeared into the December night.

Nobody thought of stopping him.

Long before Boldwood reached Casterbridge and gave himself up at the gaol, everybody was awake in the village and had heard of the murder.

CHAPTER TEN

Together at Last

Gabriel Oak was the first to enter the room and see the terrible scene. All the female guests were lined against the wall, like sheep in a storm.

As for Bathsheba, she was sitting on the floor beside the body of Troy, his head pillowed in her lap. With one hand she held a handkerchief to his breast. The other clasped his hand.

'Gabriel,' she said as if in a dream. 'Ride to Casterbridge instantly for the surgeon. It is, I believe, useless, but go. Mr Boldwood has shot my husband.'

Gabriel Oak saddled a horse and rode away. His head was full of questions.

What had happened? Where was Boldwood now? How had Troy come to be there?

When they returned three hours later, the surgeon and Oak found that Bathsheba had removed Troy to her house. He was dead, the servants said, and Bathsheba did not care what the law said. Everybody was astonished by Bathsheba's calm. She had washed Troy and dressed him in grave clothes.

Now she gave way to a fainting fit. She was put to bed and heard to moan, 'Oh, it is my fault – how can I live!'

***

A petition was taken up to plead for Boldwood's life on the grounds of insanity. During these months of waiting, Bathsheba was a shadow of the high-spirited girl she had been two years before.

At last, on a breezy March day, the verdict came: Boldwood's life was spared and he would remain in Casterbridge gaol.

Bathsheba's spirits revived, although she remained alone for most of the time. By August, she was able to walk into the village, although her cheeks were still pale, especially set against her black mourning clothes.

She visited the churchyard and gazed in satisfaction at the new inscription added to Fanny Robin's grave:

IN THE SAME GRAVE
LIE THE REMAINS OF THE AFORESAID
FRANCIS TROY,
WHO DIED DECEMBER 24th, 18–,
AGED 26 YEARS.

As she stood in the church porch, listening to the hymn sung inside, Bathsheba did not notice Gabriel Oak.

'Mr Oak,' she exclaimed. 'How long have you been here?'

'A few minutes, ma'am,' he said, respectfully.

Together they went to read the tombstone.

As they walked back to the farm, Gabriel told her that he was thinking of leaving for America the next spring.

'But it is generally assumed that you will take on Mr Boldwood's farm,' she said, astonished.

'I have had first refusal on the tenancy, that is true,' Gabriel replied, 'but nothing is settled yet.'

'And Gabriel, what shall I do without you?' Bathsheba cried. 'I do not think you should go. You have been with me so long – through bright times and dark times. I thought that if you were on my neighbouring farm, you would keep an eye on mine.'

Gabriel walked on, anxious to get away, leaving Bathsheba distressed at the news.

***

Christmas came round, and with it the end of Bathsheba's formal widowhood – and a letter from Gabriel Oak saying that he would leave her farm in the spring. Bathsheba cried bitterly over that letter.

'How will I ever go to market again?' she asked herself. 'How will I manage on my own?'

She was so distressed that she set off to see Gabriel, guided in the setting sun by pale primroses on the path. He was astonished to see her in his plain and simple cottage.

'You'll think it strange that I have come,' she began, 'but–'

'O no, not at all,' he replied.

'I cannot help but think that I have offended you,' Bathsheba said.

'No, no,' he said. 'I am not going to America. I am to become the tenant of Little Weatherbury Farm after all. I would help you, too, if it had not been for gossip in the village.'

'What gossip?' she asked.

'That I've got Boldwood's farm and soon I'll have you,' he said.

'*Have* me?' she asked.

'They mean, marry thee!' he said.

'It's too absurd,' she said. 'And too soon.'

'Too absurd,' Gabriel agreed.

'I said *too soon*,' Bathsheba explained.

Gabriel looked her long in the face, but he could not see much in the faint firelight.

'Bathsheba,' he said gently, 'if only I knew whether you would ever love me.'

'You will never know because you never ask,' she replied, laughing. 'O Gabriel, it seems as if I had come courting you.'

'And quite right, too,' he replied. 'I've danced at your heels for many a mile, my beautiful Bathsheba.'

Gabriel Oak escorted Bathsheba home. They did not talk about their love. They did not need to. Theirs was a love based on a long friendship.

Glossary

Oblong   7
A rounded, rectangular shape

Ewes   8, 13, 25
A female sheep

Grimysmock   15
A dirty, smocked linen over garment worn by an agricultural
worker

Crimson   7, 23
A rich deep red colour inclining to purple

Infatuation   32
An intense but short-lived passion or admiration for someone
or something

Conscience   33
A person's moral sense of right and wrong

Parish   19, 33
A small administrative district typically having its own church
and a priest or pastor

Also look out for:

Original by Charles Dickens
Retold by Pauline Francis

ISBN 978-1-78322-608-5

Also look out for:

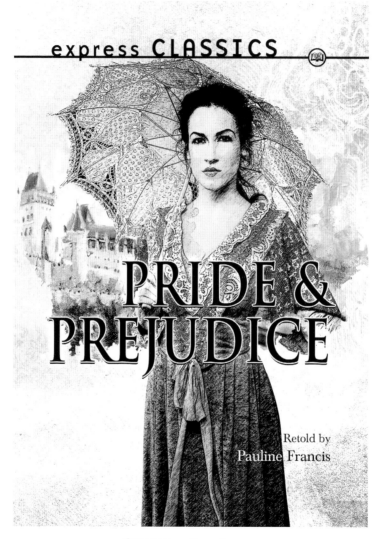

express CLASSICS

PRIDE & PREJUDICE

Retold by
Pauline Francis

ORIGINAL BY JANE AUSTEN
RETOLD BY PAULINE FRANCIS

ISBN 978-1-78322-594-1

Also look out for:

express CLASSICS

WUTHERING HEIGHTS

Retold by
Pauline Francis

ORIGINAL BY EMILY BRONTË
RETOLD BY PAULINE FRANCIS

ISBN 978-1-78322-607-8